For Manda

(I'm not sure I could have done it without you!)

First US edition 2021

First published by Nosy Crow, Ltd. (UK) 2021

Library of Congress Catalog Card Number pending

ISBN 978-1-5362-2021-6

21 22 23 24 25 26 TLF 10 9 8 7 6 5 4 3 2 1

Printed in Dongguan, Guangdong, China

This book was typeset in Goudy Infant.

The illustrations were done in pencil and colored digitally.

Nosy Crow

an imprint of

Candlewick Press

99 Dover Street

Somerville, Massachusetts 02144

www.nosycrow.com

www.candlewick.com

Ruffles

and the Red, Red Coat

David Melling

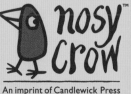

nosy crow™

An imprint of Candlewick Press

This is **Ruffles.**

Ruffles **loves** . . .

howling . . .   scratching . . .   eating . . .

fetching . . .   sniffing . . .   chewing . . .

digging . . .   running . . .   and sleeping.

But Ruffles does not love his new red coat.

Not one . . . teeny, tiny . . . little bit.

No. No. No.

No. No. **No.**

Ruffles should wear his coat
when it is cold and wet.

Today, it is cold and wet, and the rain is making puddles.

Ruffles **loves** puddles.

So Ruffles sniffs . . .   and pats . . .   and licks . . .

and splishes . . .   and splashes . . .   and sploshes . . .

and jumps . . .   and jumps . . .   and jumps . . .

without his coat.

This is Ruffles's friend Ruby!

Ruby's wearing her new blue coat!

They sniff . . .

and pat . . .

and lick . . .

and splish . . .

and splash . . .

and splosh . . .

and jump . . .

and jump . . .

and jump, until . . .

big dogs come!

The puddle is all splashed away.

And Ruffles is wet and cold and mad.

But Ruby shakes . . .   and wags her tail.   She still wants to play!

Ruffles doesn't.   No.   No.

No.   **No.**   **No.**

Now Ruby is sad.

So she goes away.

And Ruffles is all alone.

But then Ruby comes back—
with Ruffles's red coat!

It takes . . .   a really long time . . .   and he has to do . . .

lots and . . .   lots of . . .   wriggling.

Until . . .   at last . . .   The coat is on!

And look!

Another puddle!

Maybe the red coat is not so bad after all.

Ruffles loves . . .

sniffing . . .

patting . . .

licking . . .

splishing . . .

splashing . . .

sploshing . . .

and jumping . . .

in puddles . . .

but, most of all . . .

Ruffles **loves** . . .

Ruby!